TIM BURCHARD, UMPIRE

It's the worst sound I've ever heard
in all my years of umping.
Oh, I've heard plenty of pitches hit a helmet.
But this . . . this fastball, up and in.
This one hit bone, right in the face.
Not even a scream or grunt from the kid.
He went down like he was shot.

I know him.
I've umped and reffed
maybe a dozen of his games.
Not just baseball—
football and basketball, too.
The kid's a great athlete, a natural.
That's why it was such a shock to see him
go down like that.

The screams come from everywhere:
bleachers,
dugouts,
infield,
mound.

Even from me.

beanball

beanball

by gene fehler

Houghton Mifflin Harcourt
Boston • New York

The text of this book is set in 11-point Elysium Book.

The Library of Congress has cataloged
the hardcover edition as follows:
Fehler, Gene, 1940–
Beanball / by Gene Fehler.
p. cm.
Summary: Relates, from diverse points of view,
events surrounding the critical injury of a popular and
talented high school athlete, Luke "Wizard" Wallace,
when he is hit in the face by a fastball.

[1. Baseball—Fiction. 2. Sports injuries—Fiction. 3. Interpersonal relationships—
Fiction. 4. High schools—Fiction. 5. Schools—Fiction.] I. Title.
PZ7.F3318Bea 2008
[Fic]—dc22   2007013058

ISBN: 978-0-618-84348-0 hardcover
ISBN: 978-0-547-55001-5 paperback

Printed in the United States of America
DOH 10 9 8 7 6 5

4500757750

For
Polly,
Andy & Kellie,
Tim & Jacquelyn,
Mireille & Gabrielle,
with love

◆

Special thanks to
Marcia Leonard
Dinah Stevenson
Caryn Wiseman

the voices

OAK GROVE BASEBALL TEAM
Luke "Wizard" Wallace, center fielder
Andy Keller, backup infielder
Paul Gettys, pitcher
Daryl Hucklebee, coach
Gordie Anderson, outfielder
Craig Foltz, second baseman

COMPTON BASEBALL TEAM
Red Bradington, coach
Kyle Dawkins, pitcher
Dalton Overmire, shortstop
Pete Preston, catcher

OAK GROVE HIGH SCHOOL
Melody Mercer, student
Janice Trucelli, English teacher
Sarah Edgerton, student
Elaine Cotter, substitute teacher
Victor Sanderson, history teacher
Lisalette Dobbs, student

THE WALLACE FAMILY
Michelle Wallace, Luke's mother
Larry Wallace, Luke's father
Randy Wallace, Luke's grandfather
Elizabeth Wallace, Luke's grandmother

AT THE HOSPITAL
Dr. Wesley Hunter, ophthalmologist
Alice Gooding, nurse

OTHERS
Tim Burchard, umpire
Clarissa Keller, Andy's sister
Roland Zachary, baseball scout
Sally Anderson, nurse (and Gordie's mother)
Willard Kominski, baseball fan
Nancy Keller, Andy and Clarissa's mother

PART ONE

PART ONE

Luke "Wizard" Wallace and Andy Keller

"This is our year, Andy. I'm sure of it.
I had this dream last night."

"Okay, Wizard. Let's hear it."

"I dreamed it was Awards Night.
Coach Hucklebee was holding up a big trophy: State champs.
There were two little statues on top.
One was you and one was me. Co-MVPs."

"Hey, that must mean Coach picked me to start at third base."

"Sure. Why else would I have dreamed it?"

"I hope you're right.
Wait'll you hear about *my* dream.
I dreamed I was making out with Lisalette Dobbs."

"You and Lisalette? *Only* in your dreams."

"I know she's out of my league, but . . ."

"I'll say this, pal: The chances of you starting at third
and of us winning State are better than the chances
of you making out with Lisalette Dobbs."

"You think?"

3

Clarissa Keller, Andy's sister

I saw a shooting star last night.
If you see one,
you're supposed to make a wish.
So I did.

I wished that Luke and Andy would stay best friends
forever and ever.
Or at least until I'm in high school.
That would mean Luke will keep coming to our house.

I know an eleventh grader would never have
a sixth grader for a girlfriend.
I'm not dumb.
But maybe someday he'll look at me
and not just see somebody's little sister.

I hope Andy and Luke stay friends till then.

Luke "Wizard" Wallace, Oak Grove center fielder

What I love most about football
is when I jump up between two defenders
and feel the ball slap against my hands and stay there;
then I break a tackle and know that nobody can catch me.

In basketball, it's when I'm on my game,
and I know, just know,

that when the ball spins off my fingertips,
it'll hit nothing but net.

Baseball—that's the best of all.
I'm in center field, a sea of green all around me.
I see the batter swing,
and I know that if the ball is hit anywhere near me,
I'll make the catch.

I read a book about an old-time ballplayer,
Shoeless Joe Jackson.
He was such a great fielder, people called his glove
"the place where triples go to die."
Standing out in center field, I think, "That's me, too."
Nobody can ever take that feeling away.

Andy Keller, Oak Grove backup infielder

Sure I'm disappointed. Who wouldn't be?
I thought I'd be the starting third baseman.
Luke thought so, too.
But with just a few days to go before our first game,
Coach came up with this brainstorm:
Move Ricky from right field to third.

Coach figures he'll get more batting punch
if he puts Ricky at third and Julio in right,
but I think I'm as strong a hitter as either of them.
Coach has given me a fair shot;

I'm not saying he hasn't.
It's just that I haven't hit as well as I know I can.
Luke thinks I'm trying too hard,
putting too much pressure on myself.
He says I should keep my head up, that I'll get my chance.

I hope he's right.

Paul Gettys, Oak Grove pitcher

Coach has a saying: "You can't go undefeated
unless you win the first one."
I owe this win to the Wizard.
I wasn't sharp. Gave up six runs.
Didn't deserve to win.

It was in the low forties today. *Brrr.*
I like it hot.
Sweat dripping down.
My right arm as loose as an old sock.

I'd never let Coach hear me blame the cold, though.
Shoot, Coach hates excuses.
He says, "An excuse is a crutch for losers"
and "An excuse is like trying to patch
an amputated arm with a Band-Aid."
Hucklebee's a great coach,
even if he does go overboard with his cornball sayings.

Anyway, I just wasn't getting my pitches where I wanted them.
That's the whole thing.
Lucky for me, our offense pounded the ball.
Got me seven runs to work with.

Last ups, they loaded the bases with two outs.
Then a guy I should have been able to strike out
blooped one into short center.
It was a sure hit. No human could get to it.
But the Wizard—Luke Wallace—came out of nowhere
and made a sliding catch
to save the game.

I didn't deserve the win, but I'll take it.
My team came through for me.

Andy Keller, Oak Grove backup infielder

I'll take credit for Luke's nickname:
The Wizard.
Oh, yeah.
I started calling him that
'cause he's a wizard with the mitt.
I've known him since fifth grade,
and the times I've seen him drop a ball,
even in practice,
I could count on one hand.
Hey, I'd even have a few fingers left over.
He can outrun any fly ball,

and once he gets to it, it sticks to his glove
like a piece of fuzz to a sweater.

I bet there aren't many big leaguers
who can play the outfield better.

Luke "Wizard" Wallace, Oak Grove center fielder

I feel bad for Andy.
He was counting on starting,
which didn't happen,
and then he only got in for an inning
in our first game.
But he's a good ballplayer,
and this will just make him more determined.
He'll break into the starting lineup yet.
Coach is fair. He likes guys who hustle,
and nobody hustles more than Andy.
What he lacks in raw talent,
he makes up for in desire.

We've been best friends for years,
practiced together thousands of hours—
baseball, football, basketball.
The thing about him that amazes me:
I know he thinks it all comes so easy for me,
but he's never acted jealous,
not even once.

Melody Mercer, Oak Grove student

I'm going to have to decide—
who to go to prom with, I mean.
I expect at least three guys will ask me.
It's a pain, having to decide,
but I guess my problem isn't the worst one a girl can have.
I know some girls who won't get asked at all.

I don't know why anybody would want
to go steady with one boy.
High school is too early to get tied down.
Look at my mom.
She dated the same guy all through high school.
She was married at nineteen
and divorced before she was thirty.
I want to make sure I pick the right guy—
if I ever decide to get married.

I wouldn't mind going to prom with Luke.
He's the guy I've been going out with the most.
He's fun. And he likes me a lot.
I just don't know if I want to get too serious
with one of the school's biggest jocks.
That's what Mom did, and look how she ended up.
Sports were more important to Dad than Mom was.
Or me, even.

I like dating Brett. His parents are rich,
so he has plenty of money to spend on me.

I think Derek would be the best date, though.
He's absolutely gorgeous—the hottest guy in school.
He should be prom king, for sure,
and I have a good chance to be queen.
Wouldn't that make some photo?
Derek and me, all dressed up, looking beautiful together?

Janice Trucelli, Oak Grove English teacher

Luke Wallace isn't one of my top students,
only one of my favorites.
Not that I'd ever say that in public, of course.

I know he's capable of doing A work,
but it's pretty obvious he waits until the last minute
to write his essays and doesn't leave himself time
to do any revising or proofreading.

Oh, he exasperates me!
To him, the difference between an A and a B- or even a C+
isn't worth the extra effort it would take to earn the A.
He'd rather spend his time and energy on sports.

He's such fun to be around, though.
He always has a smile and a pleasant word.
He has a knack for making people feel he likes them,
and I think he truly does.

I remember during football season last fall
he kept putting off projects,
not turning in assignments on time.
I had to call his parents in for a conference,
because he was in danger of failing for the quarter.
I told them I'd never failed a student
I liked as much as I like Luke.
But if he gave me no choice, fail he would.
"Classroom obligations must be met," I told them.
Fortunately for us all, he heeded the warning.

Daryl Hucklebee, Oak Grove coach

I'm one lucky fellow, to be able to coach at Oak Grove.
Not only do they have a great baseball tradition,
but I've got a great bunch of kids to work with.
There's not one I wouldn't be proud to call my son.

Bunker Toomer was baseball coach here for nineteen years
before I took the job.
I'd coached against him and had tons of respect for him.
When he retired, he phoned me—
said I should interview here.
It's the best phone call I ever got.
I didn't know how people would react to me,
the new guy taking over for someone so loved and trusted.
But it's my third year here,
and I can't say enough about the way I've been accepted.

Maybe it's because Bunker and I
are so much alike in our coaching philosophy:
we try to make the game fun.
And if you truly *like* the kids on your team,
teach them sound, fundamental baseball,
get them to play hard,
and let them have fun,
it's a lot more likely
your team will win.

Red Bradington, Compton coach

It's too early in the season to call it a must-win game,
but, by God, it is.
It's one we have to win, just to prove to ourselves we can.

The last two years it's been Oak Grove in first place
and us in second,
and it looks like it'll be the two of us battling it out
for the conference title again this year.

By God, I'm tired of losing to Hucklebee.
He gets all the breaks, the lucky bastard.
Every call goes his way.
His players make lucky catches, get lucky hits.
Mine can hit the snot out of the ball
and it'll be right at somebody.
We're snakebit.

I'm going to throw Dawkins at them.
He's the best pitcher I've got.
We have to whip their butts,
beat that damn Hucklebee.
We just have to.
It's time for things to go our way.

Roland Zachary, baseball scout

I phoned Red Bradington, the Compton coach.
I asked him when I could see Kyle Dawkins pitch.
Dawkins is number one on my list
of high school prospects
in this part of the state.
The kid's got a big league fastball right now.
I saw him pitch twice last year,
and I had a long talk with him.
He's got the arm.
Not only that, he's got the kind of attitude
you want in a player in your organization.

Kyle Dawkins, Compton pitcher

Pro scouts came to some of my games last year.
I started getting letters from colleges, too,
wanting me to play for them.

Coach thinks I might get drafted this year
by a big league team.
I won't turn pro, though.
Not until after college.
I want that degree.
Besides, I'm not ready for pro ball.
I know that.

They tell me I've already got a big league fastball.
But that's not enough.
I need to work on my off-speed pitches
and my control.
Playing college ball will give me a chance to do that.
I gave free passes to way too many batters last year.
Heck, I walked guys who couldn't have hit my heater
if they'd swung all day.
I'm probably the main reason that what's left
of Coach Bradington's hair is turning white.

Luke "Wizard" Wallace, Oak Grove center fielder

I picked the worst time to get sick.
I don't know if it's the flu or something I ate,
but I was up half the night puking my guts out.

I tried hard to keep Mom and Dad
from hearing me in the bathroom.
Have you ever tried to puke
without making any noise?

It's not easy, let me tell you.

If they'd known I was sick,
they might have made me stay home.
And if you're not at school
on the day of a game, you can't play.

Not even the flu is going to keep me
out of a game against Compton.

Roland Zachary, baseball scout

I wasn't wrong about Dawkins.
He's got the goods.
He's wild, but most kids his age are.
Time—and someone working with him
on his mechanics—will straighten him out.

It's easy to separate the pro prospects
from the others just by the way they move.
Two that really stand out
are a couple of Oak Grove outfielders.
The way their left fielder swings the bat
is a thing of beauty.
And their center fielder—
he's fast and graceful, and he's got a rifle for an arm.

It's fun watching Dawkins compete against those two.

Luke "Wizard" Wallace, Oak Grove center fielder

A ballfield's the best medicine I know.
I've been sick as a dog since last night.
I had to run out of class third period.
I didn't even stop to get the teacher's permission,
because I thought I was going to throw up
right there at my desk.
Talk about embarrassing!
Luckily, I didn't.

Anyway, the minute I stepped onto the field this afternoon,
I felt a lot better.
Almost normal.

And now this. This is what I live for:
bottom of the seventh, our last at-bats.
Tying run on third, winning run on second.
Hitting against Kyle Dawkins,
the hardest thrower in our conference.
He's a senior now. He's fast but wild.
Last year as a sophomore, I swung against him,
and I couldn't touch his heat.
I might as well have been batting with a toothpick.

The Compton coach just came out to talk to Dawkins.
I can guess what he told him.
They don't want to risk walking me.
Dawkins's control is shaky; the last thing they want
is to have the bases loaded.
I've already pulled an inside pitch for a double,

so the smart play is for him to curve me outside.
I'll be ready for it.
I'll poke it to right, and the game will be ours.
Last week we won a game with defense in the final inning.
Today we've got a chance to win with our bats.

Andy Keller, Oak Grove backup infielder

The Wizard's the guy you want up in a situation like this.
Gordie's on deck. He's our best hitter,
both for average and power.
But in a clutch situation, Luke's the guy I want up there.

He's amazing.
For some reason—I can't explain it—
the pressure never seems to bother him.

You might think I'm biased, since Luke's my best friend.
But I could fill a book with all the times
he's come through in the clutch.
In fact, I can hardly remember a time he's failed.

Sure, Dawkins might get him out; he's got the stuff to do it.
But if I were going to bet, I'd put my money
on the Wizard.

Dalton Overmire, Compton shortstop

We've got to get him out. Come on, Dawkins.
We can't lose to Oak Grove.
But if we have to lose, I sure don't want
Wallace to be the one to beat us.

I hate that guy.

I went to school in Oak Grove for two years,
back in seventh and eighth grades.
Wallace was in most of my classes. Teacher's pet.
Couldn't do nothing wrong.
He'd pass notes or talk in class,
teachers would look the other way.

Me? Detention every time.
Back in eighth grade,
I should've gotten a starting guard spot
on the basketball team.
Instead, the coach picked Wallace, the cocky brownnose.
He got the glory; I got splinters on the bench.

The best thing about living in Compton:
I don't have to be around that guy.
Dawkins better get him out.
If he lets Wallace beat us, he'd better not sit near me
on the bus ride back home.

Red Bradington, Compton coach

This is one hell of a situation to be in.
Their best hitter's on deck, so we can't walk Wallace.
Wallace has already hammered Dawkins's fastball,
so the best bet is to bust him inside one time.
That'll move him off the plate.
Then we'll curve him away.

Dawkins's wildness doesn't give us much margin for error.
I wish I could bring somebody else in,
but he's still the best I've got.

Pete Preston, Compton catcher

Coach just told Kyle to brush Wallace back.
You kidding me?
Kyle's already walked two this inning.
We can't afford another walk.
Coach wants us to waste a pitch?
He's an idiot.
But we're still ahead, 3–2, in spite of him.

I just hope Kyle has enough sense
to ignore anything Bradington says.
I'm going to give him a target in the middle of the plate.
I hope he tries to hit it.

Even right down the gut,
Kyle's got good enough stuff to get anybody out.
Even Wallace.

Tim Burchard, umpire

It's the worst sound I've ever heard
in all my years of umping.
Oh, I've heard plenty of pitches hit a helmet.
But this . . . this fastball, up and in.
This one hit bone, right in the face.
Not even a scream or grunt from the kid.
He went down like he was shot.

I know him.
I've umped and reffed
maybe a dozen of his games.
Not just baseball—
football and basketball, too.
The kid's a great athlete, a natural.
That's why it was such a shock to see him go down like that.

The screams come from everywhere:
bleachers, dugouts, infield, mound.
Even from me.

Blood. Lots of it. It looks like Luke's dead.
"Jesus!" I yell. "Call 911!"
Then I shout to the bleachers: "We got a doctor here?"

A woman runs out to home plate.
The mother, I think, of one of the Oak Grove players.
Says she's a nurse.

Lucky for me.
Lucky for Luke.
I'm just an ump, not a doc.
I might do the wrong thing and make a bad situation worse.
It's plenty bad already.

The best I can do is hold Luke's mother,
when she runs onto the field,
try to keep her calm until the ambulance arrives.

PART TWO

PART TWO

Sally Anderson, spectator and nurse

After Luke got hit, I ran out to him.
The way he went down and lay so still,
eyes closed,
I feared the worst.
Coach Hucklebee and the umpires
were already there, but luckily no one
had tried to move him.

Someone came running from Oak Grove's dugout
with a first-aid kit.
I grabbed a pair of rubber gloves
and searched for a pulse with one hand
while trying to stop the bleeding with the other.
I was afraid Luke might choke on his own blood.

He was unconscious, so my biggest concern
was to monitor his breathing until the ambulance arrived.
Someone brought ice for his face and a jacket to cover him.
We moved people away to give him breathing room.
There was no time to think, only to react.

It wasn't until later that I remembered
my son, Gordie, was due up after Luke.

It could just as easily have been him.

Willard Kominski, longtime Oak Grove baseball fan

I've read about career-threatening and career-ending injuries
to big league players hit by pitches or batted balls:
Herb Score, Dickie Thon, Tony Conigliaro,
Don Zimmer, Bryce Florie—and worst of all,
Ray Chapman, killed by a pitch.

And I saw a kid break his leg once sliding into second.
It was a compound fracture—the bone sticking right out,
pinpoint sharp and glistening in the sun.
That was the worst thing I ever saw on a ball field.
Until now.

I still see it all in slow motion,
hear the sounds:
The pitcher shouting.
A crack, but not like when ball hits bat or helmet.
The sound of bone shattering.

Then silence. I know it lasts only for a split second,
but with Luke lying there, it seems more like an eternity
before screams come from everywhere.

Probably even from me,
but I don't remember that.

Kyle Dawkins, Compton pitcher

Oh, God! I didn't mean to hit him.
I'd walked two guys,
and Oak Grove bunted them to second and third.
That's when Coach came out
and told me to throw inside.
"Move him off the plate.
Then you can work him outside," he said.

Sure.

Like I can spot the ball wherever I want.

I should have followed Pete's lead.
He set up the target right down the middle,
and I should have thrown it there.
Not many can hit my good fastball.

Instead, I listened to Coach.
The pitch got away from me. Too far in.
I tried to shout, but there wasn't time.
I still can't believe it.
The sound.
The blood.
Wallace in the dirt.

The ambulance is gone, but I still hear the siren.
I still see Wallace's bloody face.
And look . . . my hands.
I can't stop them from shaking.

Roland Zachary, baseball scout

You always hate to see a kid get hit in the head.
You especially hate to see
a prospect like Dawkins bean someone.
Some young pitchers never recover from it.
They're afraid to pitch inside again—
and they're done.
I wonder how Dawkins will deal with it.

Michelle Wallace, Luke's mother

Somebody told me later
it took six minutes from the time Luke got hit
till the ambulance arrived.
It seemed longer.
I ran toward him.
I wanted to lift him up, hold him,
do something to help.

There was so much blood.

I remember somebody grabbing me,
holding me back, keeping me from my son.
I remember Sally bending down over Luke
for the longest time.
I remember thinking it should be me
by his side, making his pain all better,
because I'm his mother and that's what mothers are for.

But it was somebody else's mother,
and I knew I was failing him.
My little boy was covered with his own blood,
lying in the dirt in pain,
and I couldn't do a single thing to help him.

Sarah Edgerton, Oak Grove student

Luke's the only reason I came to the game.
And then to see that happen . . .
Oh, Luke!

When I moved to Oak Grove three weeks ago,
he was the first person who talked to me.
That was even before I entered the building.
"Hi," he said. "You're new, right?"
"I am," I said. "Are you the official greeter?"
I smiled at him, and he smiled back.
"Unofficial. But I keep my eyes open
for anyone who'll make our school even better
than it already is."
He looked right at me with his beautiful blue eyes.
He made me feel as if I'd already found a friend.
I hoped we'd be in some of the same classes, and we are.

The bad thing is, he's already dating someone.
A girl named Melody. She's so . . .
Well, maybe I'd like her if I knew her better.
I admit, I'm probably a little jealous.

The good thing is, last week in English
Mrs. Trucelli told us to pair up for a research project,
and Luke asked me to be his partner.
I couldn't believe it. I said yes, of course.

He didn't invite me to the baseball game,
but I'd heard kids talking about what a good player he is.
I just had to come see.

How could something like this happen?

Red Bradington, Compton coach

It's a hell of a thing,
a boy getting hit in the head like that.
But that's baseball.

Some people might blame me
for telling Dawkins to pitch him inside,
but that's part of the game.

Did I want Dawkins to hit the kid?
Hell, no.
But I'd make the same call again
in that situation.

It was a fluke, the ball getting away
from Dawkins like that.
A damn shame.

But that's baseball.
You have to play it straight.
Aggressive.
You can't back off.

A couple inches higher,
the ball hits the helmet—
maybe a harmless, glancing blow,
or, at worst, the kid gets a mild concussion.

It's a damn shame this happened,
but it's nobody's fault.

Daryl Hucklebee, Oak Grove coach

As a coach, you want nine players like the Wizard.
He can pluck a ball out of the air
the way a magician plucks a coin from someone's ear.
You see it, but you don't believe your eyes.
He could patrol big league outfields right now,
the way he handles the glove.
And hustle, attitude, desire . . .
the Wizard's got it all.

That's why it's a mystery,
him freezing on that inside pitch.
I replay it in my mind over and over—in slow motion—
the ball coming at him, and me wanting to shout,
"Look out!"

But there isn't time.
Luke doesn't move.
He just stands there
and lets the pitch take him down.

Every time I run that replay in my mind,
it turns out the exact same way.
No matter how many times I yell,
"Look out!"
I can't change the ending.

Pete Preston, Compton catcher

We won. So they say.
But it don't mean crap.
There wasn't a lot of bragging or joking around
on the bus going home.

Their coach stopped the game.
After Wallace got hit,
Hucklebee could have put in a runner for him,
and they would have had the bags loaded
with their left fielder, Anderson, up.
He's their best hitter—maybe the best in the conference.
Kyle was done. He wasn't going to face another batter,
no matter what.

But as soon as the ambulance left, Hucklebee said,
"That's all for today."

So that was the ballgame.

The only thing Coach Bradington said was,
"Three-two, us. It goes in the books as a win."

Daryl Hucklebee, Oak Grove coach

The waiting room is crowded.
I know not everyone is here because of Luke,
but a lot of people are—guys from the team,
kids from school.
Luke's parents are here,
and they're pretty shook up.
Who can blame them?

All we can do is wait. And pray.
The only real news we've heard
since Luke was brought in
is that he's alive, thank the Lord.

Nancy Keller, Andy and Clarissa's mother

The minute we got the phone call from Andy,
my husband and daughter and I came right to the hospital.
Andy had gotten a ride with somebody; he was there already.
Luke has been like a son to me for years.
I just don't know what we'll do, what Andy will do, if . . .

I see Luke's parents, Michelle and Larry.
If I feel this awful, this scared,
I can only imagine how they must feel.

Dalton Overmire, Compton shortstop

After I got home from the game,
I grabbed a bite to eat and drove to Felicia's.
Just my luck her parents were there
and she couldn't leave the house.
We didn't even have a chance to make out.

We watched a rerun of my favorite sitcom,
one of the funniest episodes ever.
Felicia's mother came in once
to see why we were laughing so hard.

Hanging out with Felicia
made me forget about Wallace
until I was driving back home.
It always made me jealous
that he got special treatment,
but I sure wouldn't trade places with him tonight.

Michelle Wallace, Luke's mother

When the doctor comes into the waiting room,
his face has the look of death.
There isn't even a hint of a smile.

Larry's arm tightens around me.
I try to prepare myself,
but I feel faint.

When he tells us they had to insert a cranial drain
to try to reduce swelling in Luke's brain,
I feel what can almost be called relief.

Dr. Wesley Hunter, ophthalmologist

It's touch-and-go, but we reduced the swelling.
There's still danger of further hemorrhaging,
but we stabilized him for now.
We have to wait to do further surgery.

A key concern is whether he'll lose his sight.
There's no hope for the left eye;
the damage is too massive.
The question now is: Can we save the right eye?

The next several hours are critical.

Larry Wallace, Luke's father

The doctors still don't know
when Luke will regain consciousness.
Or even *if* he will.

He's got a lot of broken facial bones.
The eye specialist, Dr. Hunter, talked to us.
He said something about an orbital fracture.
He said he was concerned about what he called
"a vitreous and possibly retinal hemorrhage."
I'm not sure exactly what that means.
All I know is that it doesn't sound good.

They can't operate yet.
They have to reduce the swelling first.
The hardest thing is just sitting here waiting.
I want to know that they're doing something.
I want to do something.
But the only thing I can do
is pace and sit and pace and sit some more
and keep asking why this had to happen.

Luke, my boy.
Please, God.
Please.

Randy Wallace, Luke's grandfather

Elizabeth and I set out the second we got the call.
We live almost three hours from Oak Grove—
with normal driving, that is.
We made it a lot quicker tonight.
In fact, it's surprising I didn't get a speeding ticket.
Not that I was even worried about that.

I still can't believe it's Luke
whose life is on the line.
I had a health scare last year—
had to have quadruple bypass surgery.
It turned out fine. No complications.
I'm exercising now and feeling better
than I have in years.

When I was in the hospital,
I could tell that Luke was worried about me.
I told him, "Don't you fret.
I give you my firm promise:
I'm going to be around to see you play in the big leagues."

Luke was scared I was going to up and die on him.
Now here I am, strong as a horse, afraid for Luke.
Go figure.

Elizabeth Wallace, Luke's grandmother

My husband, Randy, is crazy about sports.
If he's not out playing golf, he's watching it on TV.
That and baseball, football, hockey, basketball,
and . . . well . . . just about everything else.
I've never shared his interest,
and our two daughters never played sports.
They're both married, but so far
only our son, Larry, has given us a grandchild: Luke.
Now I'm hoping that if our daughters ever do have kids,
they won't encourage them to play sports.

Luke's like his father and grandfather:
sports mean everything to him.
I'll attend any school or church program
Luke is in—plays or music, things like that.
But I skip his games.
He knows I love him and I'm happy for him
in whatever he does.
I just don't enjoy watching sports,
and the men in my life accept that.

Even after all these years of being around such ardent fans,
I've never understood the hold sports has on them.

Now I understand it even less.

Willard Kominski, longtime Oak Grove baseball fan

I couldn't sleep.
So I got up around midnight
and tried to watch some TV,
but I couldn't concentrate.
I kept seeing that scene at home plate.

Now the red numbers on my digital clock
are flashing a bright 2:14,
and I'm still seeing Luke on the ground.
That image keeps blocking out everything else.

My wife passed three years ago.
The hardest part of being alone is nights like this.

Luke "Wizard" Wallace

Why is everything black?
Am I dreaming?
I want to pinch myself and wake up,
but my arms are too heavy to move.
My throat's dry.
It's hard to swallow.
What kind of dream is this?

The throbbing.
Where am I?

This doesn't feel like my bed.
So tired.
Sleep.
I need to sleep again,
to wake up from this dream.
This . . .

Alice Gooding, nurse

I've been working on the surgical floor six years now.
You'd think after all this time
I wouldn't get so torn up by the sight
of purple disfigured faces
half hidden beneath mounds of gauze,
of kids teetering on that slim fence
between life and death,
of families waiting for news
that all too often brings them to tears
or, even worse, sets off wails that echo
up and down the halls.

But this boy . . .
I know him. I know his family.
I see them at church sometimes.
I don't go often—most weekends I work.
But when I go, I always see them there.

Michelle, Larry, Luke . . . I know them.
That's why this case seems worse to me than most.

PART THREE

PART THREE

Sarah Edgerton, Oak Grove student

Nobody's called me with news about Luke.
Not that I expected anyone to.
It's not as if I'm a close friend.

I want to talk to somebody. Who might know?
The hospital? Coach Hucklebee? Andy Keller?
They'll know at school tomorrow.
I don't feel like going, but I will—
just so I can find out about Luke.
He has to be all right. He just has to.

But I'm scared.
I watched him every second
from the time the ball hit him
until the ambulance took him away,
and he never moved.

Not once.

Dalton Overmire, Compton shortstop

If Kyle's pitch had killed Wallace, we would've heard by now.
But nobody here at school seems to know what's happened.

I couldn't stand the guy, but I don't want him dead.
I don't want anybody thinking that.
What happened to him,

I wouldn't wish on anybody.
As much as I hate the guy,
I felt bad seeing him lying there like that.
I really did.

Janice Trucelli, Oak Grove English teacher

I didn't hear about what had happened to Luke
until I got to school today.
I could tell right away something was wrong.
Faces were grim. Everybody seemed to move in slow motion.

"What's going on? What's the matter?" I asked.

"You haven't heard? Luke Wallace. He died last night."

I've never fainted in my life,
but I almost collapsed then.
I felt lightheaded. My legs started to melt.
I had to sit down.
Not Luke! Not that dear boy!

I don't know how the rumor got started or who started it,
but it was another ten or fifteen minutes
before I learned that he was alive—
in critical condition, but alive.

Sometimes, when I don't have a ton of essays to grade,
or when I don't have some meeting or activity after school,

I'll stop by and watch a game.

I'm glad I wasn't at yesterday's game.
It's hard enough just hearing about what happened;
seeing it would have been so much worse.

Elaine Cotter, Oak Grove substitute teacher

This was my first day subbing at Oak Grove High.
Never again.
Not at that school.
Not for the kind of money a sub gets paid.
Not that they'd ever ask me back anyway.

I've never had a class as unresponsive
as that first-period class.
Some subs just sit and give kids study time.
I like to actually teach,
and I'm good at it. I am.

I know it takes a while for kids to wake up in the morning,
especially eleventh graders.
So I tried to liven things up with humor.
Most of them wouldn't even fake a smile.
One boy was so rude, I ran from the room
before they could see my tears.

I should have stood up to him, but I couldn't.
I just . . . couldn't.

Craig Foltz, Oak Grove second baseman

That damn substitute teacher cost me two days' detention.
I guess I'm lucky it wasn't worse.
Principal Jenks cut me some slack.

The sub was up there joking around, a goofy grin on her face.
Luke is in the hospital fighting for his life,
and here's this dumb woman trying to get laughs.
I should have kept my mouth shut,
but finally I just couldn't take it.
I slammed my book and yelled,
"Hey, lady! This isn't the damn comedy channel.
We're supposed to be learning something.
Just teach, if you know how.
Your jokes aren't even funny."

She got this shocked look, like I'd punched her in the gut.
She grabbed her purse and ran out.
Didn't even look back.

I knew I was screwed.
I figured I'd get called to Jenks's office.
Instead, he came to our room. Alone.
And stayed with us until the bell.

Luke "Wizard" Wallace

My face.
Sometimes it's on fire.
Sometimes it's not even there.
Do I have a nose?
Lips?
Eyes?
I can't see.
I can't even raise my eyebrows.

My whole head feels like my mouth does
when the dentist gives me Novocain.
I dream that the pain wakes me up,
but then everything's numb.
And I sleep again.

Janice Trucelli, Oak Grove English teacher

It's been two days since Luke got hurt.
Hallways are still quiet.
There's less laughing and roughhousing than normal.
Faces are solemn.
No one knows yet if Luke will pull through,
or, if he does, what kind of damage there might be.

When Luke was here, it seemed I was always chastising him
for speaking out of turn or joking at inappropriate times.

I only wish I were able to do it today.

Clarissa Keller, Andy's sister

Luke's been in the hospital two days now.
Andy went to visit him right after baseball practice,
and he took me with him.
But they wouldn't let us see Luke.

He's in the ICU—that means intensive care unit.
They operated on him again today.
They're saying he's in critical condition.
That means there's still a chance he could die.

I wish they'd let me see him.
Maybe what he needs is just for someone
to be there with him and hold his hand
so he knows how much somebody cares about him.

Andy Keller, Oak Grove backup infielder

Clarissa and I tried to see Luke, but they wouldn't let us.
Since we couldn't see him, we didn't stay long.
I had to do some serious studying
for a test about World War II.

We've spent the past few weeks
on a unit called "The United States at War."
We talked in class about how boys
not much older than we are
fought and died in wars.

Until then, most of us hadn't thought much
about casualties.
It was as if they were just numbers in a history book.
Not real people.
We were all going to live forever.

Right.

Luke "Wizard" Wallace

Is it morning or night?
It feels like morning, but I don't think it is.
I kind of remember Mom and Dad
talking to me today.
Or was it yesterday?
A doctor, too. I'm not sure, though.
Maybe I just dreamed it.
But it seemed too real for a dream.

What is real?
I bet what I thought was a dream was actually real:
I was trying to run barefoot on the beach,
but it wasn't sand, it was marshmallows.
Melting, sticky, burning-hot marshmallows.
I tried to pull my feet out, but I fell face first
into more red-black globs of marshmallows.
Some got stuck in my throat.
I couldn't breathe for the longest time.

My face still burns.
My throat's still sore.
Sore and dry.
From the marshmallows?

Kyle Dawkins, Compton pitcher

I turned in my uniform today.
Coach was furious.
I listened to him rant for a while; then I left.
He just doesn't get it.
He doesn't know what it feels like to throw a fastball
that can bust a kid's head open.
The thought of facing another batter
scares me too much to do it again.

"You've got colleges and pro scouts looking at you," he said.
"You'd be a damn fool to give that up.
You owe it to your school to pitch," he said.
"We can win the conference with you pitching.
Don't make a rash decision," he said.
"Give it a few days."

I didn't try to explain that baseball's a game,
not life or death.
At least it shouldn't be.

He wouldn't understand.
For him, it's all about winning.

Take our "victory" against Oak Grove.
Coach says it's a win; it sure doesn't feel like one to me.
I thought they might call it a suspended game
and have the two teams finish it later,
but I guess they're not doing that.

When I put my uniform on Coach's desk,
all clean and folded,
I didn't leave my guilt with it.
But I felt fifty pounds lighter,
and I could breathe normally again,
and my hands weren't shaking.

Pete Preston, Compton catcher

At practice today, Coach told us Kyle had left the team.
It would be an understatement to say he was pissed.
He all but called Kyle a quitter.
I already knew what Kyle had done.
He'd phoned me the night before
and told me he was turning in his uniform.
I didn't try to talk him out of it.
Maybe someday he'll be ready to pitch again,
but not now.
No way.

All Coach cares about is wins.
If he gave a damn about Kyle,
he'd worry that he hasn't been to school since it happened—

except to turn in his uniform.
I phone Kyle a couple times every day now,
because I'm afraid he might do something to hurt himself.
He's got me scared as hell.
It's as if the ball had hit *him,*
as if it had smashed *him* up inside
just as bad as it smashed Wallace's face.

I was closest to Wallace when he got hit.
I heard the bones shatter.
I saw his bloody face.
Maybe Coach can forget about it
and pretend it doesn't matter,
that it's just part of the game.
But it does matter. It has to.

If it doesn't matter, we're all in big trouble.

Red Bradington, Compton coach

If we could play that last inning over, I'd rather
Wallace had gotten a hit and Oak Grove had beaten us.
I wish I'd put him on base
and taken my chances with Anderson.
At least then we'd have Dawkins for the rest of the season.

I can't believe the kid quit on me,
quit on his teammates.

Now I have to figure out which of my other pitchers
can pick up the slack, get us those wins
I was counting on from Dawkins.

We can still do it,
but the kid just made my job
a hell of a lot tougher.

Andy Keller, Oak Grove third baseman

I started at third today against Palo Cove.
My first start.
Coach moved Julio from right to left
and Gordie from left to center.
Ricky went back to right field.

I'd been hoping I could break into
the starting lineup, but not this way.
I felt guilty going out there.
If Luke hadn't gotten hurt, I'd still be on the bench.

I did okay.
Fielded three grounders cleanly.
Coach hit me eighth.
I didn't get any hits, but it didn't hurt us.
We still won, 7–3.

Michelle Wallace, Luke's mother

Luke talked to us today,
thank the Lord.

It's been three days of waiting, of watching him,
unrecognizable beneath the thick white bandages.

Three days of doctors working to stop the swelling,
to repair fractured bones in his face.

Three days without hearing his voice,
of wondering if he would live through the surgeries.

Three days of prayer,
never certain if God was even listening.

Luke "Wizard" Wallace

They say I've been here for three days.
I had no idea.
Today is the first day that doesn't seem like a dream.

I try to picture how it happened.
Dawkins was in his stretch, I remember that.
I can see him looking in at me or at his catcher.
That's the last I remember.
I don't remember seeing the ball at all,
or even getting hit.

When I woke up in the hospital the first time,
I had no clue why I was here.
All I knew is what people told me.
When I was finally able to mouth some words,
I asked them about the game.
They told me Coach stopped it,
gave the win to Compton.

He shouldn't have done that.
Gordie was up next.
We'd have won it, for sure.

Dr. Wesley Hunter, ophthalmologist

It's always a tough decision:
Tell the good news first—
or the bad news?

The good news:
Luke's gotten through the most dangerous time.
It was touch-and-go those first few hours.
Dr. Yang was on call in the ER.
He had to insert a cranial drain
to reduce the swelling in Luke's brain.
Luke almost didn't survive the night.
The bleeding and swelling seem under control now.
He appears to be out of danger
with no apparent brain damage.

The bad news:
Splintered orbital bones make for a long
and painful recovery time.
Worse still, we won't be able
to save the sight in Luke's left eye.

Larry Wallace, Luke's father

How can we tell Luke?
It'll kill him.
How can we tell him he'll have sight in only one eye?
All he's worked for, all he's dreamed of,
his whole future—gone.

I shouted at the doctor.
I demanded to know what they'd done wrong.
I tried to get them to tell me there was something
they could do to save Luke's sight.
Was everybody in that hospital incompetent?

It took a few hours before I could think straight
and apologize for how I'd acted, for the things I'd said.
If *I* can't control my rage, what can I expect from Luke
when he hears those words:
"blind in one eye"?

We'll all be there when the doctor tells him.
We'll all be there when he learns
that his life has changed forever.

Michelle Wallace, Luke's mother

I feel like a hypocrite, Lord.
Forgive these thoughts I've been having.
It's just that I suddenly have a hard time believing
the lessons I've preached
to my Sunday school classes all these years.

It's easy to believe, in the abstract,
that You're always with us,
that You meet our every need.
If somebody else's son were being operated on,
I'd tell his family, "Just have faith.
God is with you. He'll make everything all right."
But it's *my* son, and what if You can't,
or won't, make everything all right?

How can I face my class again?
What can I possibly tell them
that I don't, deep down, feel is a lie?
Help me understand.

I know I don't deserve to ask You to heal Luke.
But Luke's deserving. He is.
I'm begging You: Please help him.

Luke "Wizard" Wallace

They acted like it was good news
when they told me I'd be blind in one eye.
They had these smiles pasted on.
Good news.
Sure.

After they left,
I had all night to lie here thinking
about how I've lost everything.
The pills they gave me finally made me sleep,
but I even dreamed about what blindness would be like.

While I'm here, they might as well cut off an arm or leg.
Without depth perception, you can't hit a baseball
or catch one, either.
College basketball is out.
Football? I don't know.
With only one good eye,
is it possible to run the ball
and sense the exact moment your blocker
gives you the smallest of openings to shoot through?
Is it possible to make a crisp block?
Or catch a pass?

There's hardly been a school day in years
when I haven't had practice or a game in some sport.
What now?
I don't think I could stand just watching the games,
knowing I should be out there playing.

"Be thankful you're alive."
I'll scream if I hear that again.
I swear I will.
Doesn't anybody know there's a big difference
between being alive and *living?*

Larry Wallace, Luke's father

Great news!
The doctor says if there are no complications,
Luke can be moved from the ICU tomorrow.

It's the most encouraging thing that's happened
since Luke got here.

Craig Foltz, Oak Grove second baseman

My old man doesn't work Saturdays,
so he let me take his truck.
I figured it was time I saw Luke.
I owed him that much.
It was my fault he got hurt.

I booted a ball in the sixth.
Cost us two runs.
We shouldn't even have had to bat in the seventh.

If they hadn't told me it was him in that bed,
I wouldn't have known by looking.
His face was almost all wrapped in bandages.
The part that wasn't covered was purple as a grape.

I don't know who had more trouble
trying to talk,
him or me.

PART FOUR

PART FOUR

Andy Keller, Oak Grove third baseman

Hey, I'd gladly give up sight in one of my eyes
if it meant that Luke could have his sight back.
I mean it.

I know what you're thinking:
that it's easy for me to make the offer
when I know it can't happen,
that I'll never actually have to put up or shut up.

But it's clear Luke needs two eyes more than I do.
The best I'll ever be in sports
is a decent high school athlete.
I don't have the speed or the size or the talent
to go beyond that. I accept that.
The only reason I'm even as good as I am,
is because I've played with and against Luke for years.
He's made me better.
There are limits, though, and I've about reached mine.
You can't turn a hamburger into a T-bone steak.
I'm about as good right now as I can expect to get.

Luke has the talent be a college or even a pro star
in any one of three sports.
But he can't do it with just one eye.
Nothing would make me happier
than to be able to trade
one of my good eyes for Luke's bad one.

Melody Mercer, Oak Grove student

I went to the hospital to visit Luke.
Not because I wanted to.
I hate hospitals.
The disgusting smells.
The creepy sounds.
The old people ready to die everywhere you look.

But Jennifer, Heather, and Caitlin kept asking me
if I'd gone to see him—
like, just because I've been dating him,
I'm obligated or something.
They wouldn't be so quick to go if it was *their* boyfriend
lying there all gross looking.

My stomach started doing little flips
when I saw his face.
I thought I'd barf right there.
And trying to talk to him was awful.
I was in his room for maybe two minutes.
It felt like an hour.

Daryl Hucklebee, Oak Grove coach

Andy Keller's got some big shoes to fill.
Of course, trying to replace a kid like the Wizard
is darn near impossible.
It would put way too much pressure on the boy

for anybody to expect that of him.
But what Andy lacks in physical skills,
he makes up for in hustle and desire and smarts.
He's a lot like Luke in that regard.
That's what made my decision
to go with Ricky at third to start the season
such a tough one.

Andy's as good with the glove as Ricky,
just not as good a hitter.
I'd like for him to get around a bit quicker
on the fastball, but hey,
there aren't many kids I can't say that about.

Gordie Anderson, Oak Grove center fielder

I don't think I've ever made a better catch
than the one I made in today's game.
I ran deep into left center,
and right before I got to the fence,
I leaped and made a backhand catch.
I can't believe I even got to the ball.
The fact that I caught it surprised me more than anybody.

Anyway, when I came off the field after the inning was over,
Andy was waiting for me by third base.
He grinned and said,
"You looked like the Wizard out there!"
The second the words were out,

he got this look on his face
like he'd said something he shouldn't have.
His smile disappeared and he muttered, "Well, almost."

Sarah Edgerton, Oak Grove student

Today I saw Luke for the first time since his accident.
I hardly recognized him.
I don't know what I expected.
After seeing his face covered with blood that terrible day,
I should have known he'd look bad.

At school he always seemed to be smiling.
He didn't smile once today.
I don't know if it's because he can't
or because he just didn't want to.

I told him how much everybody misses him
and how anxious we were that he come back soon.
I told him I'd keep him updated
on our research project.
I said he should let me know if he needed anything—
class notes, assignments, things like that.
It was hard trying to carry on a conversation
because he didn't say much,
mostly just Yes, No, Okay, Thanks.

I wish I could have done something
or said something
to make him feel better.

Luke "Wizard" Wallace

Sarah Edgerton came to visit me today.
I was really surprised; I barely know her.
About the only time I'd ever talked to her before
was when we started working together
on our research project for English.
I asked her to be my partner and she agreed.
Actually, I'd wanted Melody to be my partner.
We've dated a lot lately, and I figured
it would give me a chance
to spend time in school with her.
But she paired up with Heather Sullivan.
I thought if I asked another girl to team up with me,
it might make Melody jealous.
Sarah was the only girl I could find
who didn't already have a partner.

My plan didn't work, though;
Melody didn't seem to mind.

Andy Keller, Oak Grove third baseman

I guess Gordie's come to see Luke
more times than anybody else from the team—
besides me, that is.
He's got a great bedside manner.
Most other guys get all nervous
when they try to talk to Luke.

Gordie says things like, "You know, Wizard,
it's your fault I'm so worn out these days.
Now that you're not out there,
I have to run twice as far
to cover the whole outfield."

He doesn't seem spooked by Luke's face
the way most everybody else is.
He jokes around and tries to lift Luke's spirits.

It's just too bad he hasn't had
any more luck at it than I've had.

Gordie Anderson, Oak Grove center fielder

Ma's been a home healthcare nurse
since before I was born.
She took me with her a lot when I was a little kid
and she couldn't get a baby sitter,
so I've been around sick people practically my whole life.
I've seen things a heck of a lot worse than Luke's face.

He probably wonders why
more guys don't come to visit him.
It's not that they don't care.
It's not that they don't wish
the whole thing had never happened
and he was back playing again.

Some of the guys just can't handle
seeing him lying there helpless
with his face looking like something
out of a monster flick.

They might be doing Luke a favor by staying away.

Clarissa Keller, Andy's sister

Luke's been feeling so bad,
and he doesn't like the hospital food much,
so I decided to make him something special.
I decided to make him some brownies.

I didn't ask Mom to help me;
I wanted to do this all by myself.

I had to throw the first batch out
because they were dry and half burnt.
The second batch was better.

Luke ate three big brownies
in the few minutes I was in his room,
so even though he didn't say so,
I know he liked them.

Luke "Wizard" Wallace

Clarissa is sweet.
She usually comes along with Andy,
but sometimes she comes alone.
She knows how to cheer me up,
if only with her smile and her cute dimples.
Sure, Andy and I complain
about what a pest she is sometimes,
but she's really a pretty neat kid.

I don't have any brothers or sisters,
but if I had a sister,
I'd want her to be like Clarissa.

Actually, I spend so much time at Andy's,
I sometimes feel as though she *is* my sister.

Andy Keller, Oak Grove third baseman

I've never hit better.
I can't explain it.
In the last three games, I'm seven for ten,
two of them doubles.
I can't remember ever getting seven hits
in a three-game stretch,
even in Little League.

I wish Luke could've been there.

He'd be proud of the way I'm hitting.
He'd be proud of the way the team is playing.
He has to know we're doing it for him.
We owe it to him to win the conference.
The way he played, his love for the game
made everybody around him play better.

We remember, and we don't want to let him down.

Luke "Wizard" Wallace

The doctors say it'll be a while yet
before I can go home.
I still have one more operation to get through,
and I can't go home until after the surgery,
because if I move around much
before the bones are completely set,
I'll run the risk of losing sight in my right eye, too.
They say there's no chance I'll ever see again
from my left eye.
None.
The surgery is only to make sure there's no further damage.

Maybe they're saying that so I don't get my hopes up.
Maybe when they operate they'll discover
a way to save my sight after all.
Maybe there *is* a chance.

Melody Mercer, Oak Grove student

Andy Keller stopped me in the hall today.
He actually sounded mad because I hadn't been
to the hospital to visit Luke again.
Like it's my duty to go.
I don't think so!

I'm sorry Luke got hurt; he's a nice guy.
But it's not like we're an item or anything.
So we dated a few times. So what?
We had fun, but there's nothing serious between us.
That one visit to the hospital was enough.
The place is so depressing,
and there wasn't anything for us to talk about.

I'll see him when he gets home from the hospital.
It'll be easier then.

Red Bradington, Compton coach

It's not the same team without Dawkins.
We need his arm.
I had no choice but to pitch Klinghagen today.
Sometimes he throws well in batting practice,
but in a game . . . I don't know. He chokes.
That's about the truth of it.
He was tossing lollipops up there,
and the Crescentville players were sure taking their licks.

When you have a kid hit three home runs,
like Preston did for us today,
and your team scores eleven runs,
you should win the damn game.

Good defense is the only reason
Crescentville didn't score more than their fourteen.

A coach can make all the right moves,
but if he doesn't have the horses . . .

Luke "Wizard" Wallace

The days are so long.
The only thing that helps me get through them
is when people come to visit.

Mom and Dad, Andy and Clarissa,
Gordie, Coach, and Sarah Edgerton.
They're the ones who've been here most.
I keep hoping Melody will come again.
Just seeing her pretty face
and being able to touch her
would give me something to think about
during the long nights.

Sometimes I feel like I'm trapped on a desert island.
Once in a while a ship comes in.
But not to save me.

Not to take me away.
A visitor shows up and then leaves.
The ship sails into the sunset,
and I'm alone again.

Andy Keller, Oak Grove third baseman

I've never seen Luke so down.
He's got good enough reason, that's for sure.
Before the accident, we'd always joke around.
Even when he was in the dumps because of a tough loss
or because he hadn't played as well as he thought he should,
I could always cheer him up.
But not today.

I told him this story:
In history class we were doing a review
for our big exam on U.S. wars.
Mr. Sanderson asked Gilda Roumaine about the War of 1812,
when and where the final battle was fought.
Gilda said she didn't remember where,
but she thought the year was 1776.

Luke didn't even smile.

Dr. Wesley Hunter, ophthalmologist

Given the crisis we were faced with that first night—
the possibility of total blindness,
brain damage,
or even death—
I couldn't be happier with Luke's progress.
Physically, at least.

I know Luke doesn't agree.
Anything short of being able to see
with both eyes is unacceptable to him.
But his final surgery went well.
If there are no complications,
in a few weeks he should be able to resume
normal activity without fear of further damage.

Luke "Wizard" Wallace

I almost wish I were deaf instead of half blind.
Then I wouldn't have to listen
to people's stupid remarks.
They come to visit me,
and I hear pity in their voices.
Those who don't feel sorry for me tell me
how thankful I should be to be alive.
They remind me that so many others
have it a lot worse than I do.

Of course they do. I know that.
There are kids dying of cancer
right in this hospital.
There are kids without arms or legs,
kids who are completely blind.

But playing sports has been my life,
and now that's been taken away.
I *understand* that I should be thankful;
I just can't *feel* thankful.

Victor Sanderson, Oak Grove history teacher

We've covered a lot of information in our unit on war.
I thought a good way to personalize its tragedies
would be to read the class some poems on the subject.
Two that I shared were written by Wilfred Owen.
He knew about the horrors of combat firsthand.
He was a soldier in World War I
and was killed a week before it ended—
a young man in his midtwenties,
with an unlimited future ahead of him.

In his poem "Disabled," he writes about
a legless young man in a wheelchair.
Toward the end of the poem, there are two lines:
"Tonight he noticed how the women's eyes
Passed from him to the strong men that were whole."
When I read them, Sarah Edgerton burst into tears.

She covered her face and ran out of the room.

I wish more of my students showed emotion
at the reading of moving and powerful poems,
especially about the tragedies attendant to war.

Owen surely would have been gratified by her reaction.

Luke "Wizard" Wallace

It's hell being a prisoner in this bed.
If I move too much, my head aches so bad,
I feel like screaming.

I'm going crazy just lying here.
I remember how it feels
to run as fast as I can,
my legs weightless, my head clear,
my breath coming quick and easy.
I remember how it feels
to know I can run forever and nobody can catch me.
Nothing can touch me.
Nothing can stop me from getting where I'm going,
ahead of everyone else.

Now I'm stuck in this bed,
and I feel like a turtle turned upside down,
trapped inside a shell,
when all I want to do is run free.

Melody Mercer, Oak Grove student

Wait till you see my prom dress.
It's so cool!
I know Derek will think it's sexy.
I've already told him what color corsage he should get me.
I know we'll be the most gorgeous couple there.
Everyone says we'll be voted king and queen.

I'll just die if we aren't!

Luke "Wizard" Wallace

I've been fooling myself.
I kept telling myself it was all a mistake,
that they'd find some way to save my left eye.
But now I know the sight's gone forever.

The weird thing is,
I don't feel angry or sad.
All I feel is a big hole inside me,
an emptiness that can't be filled.
It's as if I'm hollow—
one of those chocolate Easter bunnies
you break open and find

nothing's there.

Andy Keller, Oak Grove third baseman

I'm taking Peggy Arrons to prom.
She's a lot more excited about it than I am.
To be honest, the thought of going
doesn't really thrill me.

Luke and I were supposed to double-date.
He probably would have gone with Melody Mercer.
I hear she's going with Derek Hamilton.
Talk about a guy who loves himself.
He and Melody deserve each other, if you ask me.
But I don't dare say that to Luke.
He's kind of blind when it comes to Melody.
Damn! What made me say that?

Prom won't be much fun without Luke.
It's not right, the rest of us out partying all night
and him stuck in that hospital room.

The guy I really envy is Garrett Davis.
He's going with Lisalette Dobbs.
Some people have all the luck.

Luke "Wizard" Wallace

I had the TV on for a while this afternoon.
I've never been home much during the day,
so I had no idea how bad the shows are.

I kept flipping through the channels.
Nothing.
The sports channels reminded me of too many things
I didn't want to think about.
The talk shows were filled with people
who spent all their time screaming at each other.
The soaps were depressing.
I wasn't in the mood to hear about
all the problems the characters thought they had.

Finally, I found a movie, an old western, that wasn't too bad.
But after a few minutes, my head started to ache again,
so I turned if off and tried to sleep.

Elizabeth Wallace, Luke's grandmother

Larry and Randy encouraged Luke's sports.
I don't fault them.
That's what fathers and grandfathers
do with sons and grandsons.

But I thought there should be more balance.
I tried to interest Luke in real music—
Chopin, Bach, and Mozart—
not the kind of music so many teenagers listen to:
loud, screaming cacophony.

A few months ago, Luke played me some songs
by his favorite group, the Cave People.

It was just noise to me,
but Luke is my grandson,
so I pretended to like it.

I teach piano, and when Luke was young,
I gave him lessons for three years.
He decided he'd rather practice baseball.
I think that's a shame.
There comes a time when people can't play sports.
Music lasts forever.

Luke "Wizard" Wallace

I wonder if Mom told Grandma
it's prom night.
Grandma drove all the way over to see me,
and she gave me the new Cave People CD
I've been meaning to buy.
She said, "I asked your mother,
and she said you don't have this one."

Grandma is cool.
She stayed for a long time
and listened to the whole CD with me.

Sarah Edgerton, Oak Grove student

I didn't go to prom. Nobody asked me.
I doubt that Luke would have,
even if he'd been in school.
There are lots of other girls he would have asked
before he even considered me.

Daddy always tells me I'm smart and funny and pretty.
He has to say that. That's his job as a father.
He wondered why I wasn't going to the prom.
He thought I should have lots of guys inviting me.

I told him it was because
I haven't been at Oak Grove long enough
to get to know anyone.
That's not it, though.
I just can't bring myself to go up to a boy
the way some girls do
and flirt and make him feel important.
I can't play that game,
and I don't want to.

Jenny Lipton told me Carl Scruggins likes me,
but I guess he couldn't work up the nerve to ask me.
He's even quieter than I am.
It probably would have been the quietest date in history.

I don't know if I would have said yes.
I might have,
just to be able to say I went to my junior prom.

Andy Keller, Oak Grove third baseman

Some prom.
I wasn't very excited about going in the first place.
Now I wish I hadn't spent all that money.
Peggy danced more with Lanny Carpenter
than she did with me.

The girl Lanny brought, Dana Travors,
spent most of the night sitting alone.
I bet she wasn't too happy, either.

If this were a movie, Peggy would have left with Lanny,
and I would have left with Dana,
and all four of us would have had a great night.

But it wasn't a movie.

Willard Kominski, longtime Oak Grove baseball fan

The team's playing better than I expected.
When Luke Wallace got hurt,
I figured Oak Grove would just lie down and die.
But the opposite is true.
The kids are playing with intensity,
with fire.
They might even go all the way to State.

Luke "Wizard" Wallace

I'm happy the team is winning.
But I'd be lying if I said it didn't hurt
knowing the team can win without me.
Doesn't everybody want to feel he's indispensable?
Or at least missed?

Sarah Edgerton, Oak Grove student

Sometimes I wonder if Luke
even wants me to come see him.
He's so quiet—
not at all the way he was before he got hurt.
It's mostly a monologue when I'm there.
I try to be upbeat.
I try to talk about funny things
that happened at school.
He doesn't seem interested.

Each time I go to the hospital,
I tell myself that my being there
will help cheer him up,
but it doesn't seem to.
Each time I leave, I tell myself I'm not going back.
But I do.
I say I'm doing it for him.
Am I just kidding myself?

Luke "Wizard" Wallace

I was surprised the first time Sarah visited me.
I'm surprised she keeps coming back;
I know I'm not good company.
It's not *her* fault I don't feel much like laughing.

The first few times she came, I wished she was Melody.
It's pretty clear Melody's not coming back,
and now, I have to admit,
I kind of look forward to Sarah's visits.
She's got a nice smile and a great sense of humor.
She always tells me funny things
that have happened at school.
A few of them I've already heard about,
from either Gordie or Andy,
but the way she tells a story makes it seem funnier.

Here's an example:
Principal Jenks gives the morning announcements.
He's got a high-pitched voice you wouldn't expect
from somebody as big as he is,
and he always ends the announcements
with a quote from a famous person.
Some of the quotes are so dumb,
everyone in homeroom groans.

Anyway, Sarah's got his voice down cold,
so when she imitates him
giving one of his dumb quotes,
it almost makes me laugh.

I know Sarah's trying to make me feel better.
I guess she kind of does.

Sarah Edgerton, Oak Grove student

I don't know if I should have done it, but I did.
I printed a bunch of articles off the Internet
and sent them to Luke—anonymously.
I don't know how he'll take the information,
and I don't want him to be mad at me.
It's just that I can see how depressed he is.
I thought the articles might help.

They're about people who are successful in sports
even though each of them has vision in only one eye.
There's a professional hockey player,
a college baseball pitcher, and a lot of others.

I want Luke to know he doesn't have to give up
the things he loves because he's lost an eye.
I want to do something to bring his smile back.

Luke "Wizard" Wallace

I got an envelope today . . . full of articles
about athletes who still compete,
even though they're blind in one eye.

I didn't realize it was possible.
I read them over and over,
until I was too tired to read anymore.

Later on, I realized
there was no name on the envelope,
so I don't know who sent the articles.
My first thought was Coach Hucklebee.
But he would have given them to me in person.
He would have talked to me about them.
Same with Mom or Dad or Andy.

What was he thinking, the guy who sent them?
Why was he afraid to let me know?
Did he think I'd be pissed, that I'd cuss him out
and tell him to mind his own business?

Would I have done that?
Have I been that nasty to people,
that hard to talk to?

Alice Gooding, nurse

When I went into Luke's room, he was reading.
He's supposed to avoid eyestrain,
but some reading is okay.
I asked him if it was a school assignment,
and he didn't answer.
Then, when I said it was time to change his dressings,

I realized he hadn't even noticed I was there—
he'd been so engrossed in what he was reading.

The next time I went to his room, he was asleep.
A sheet of paper was still in his hand.

PART FIVE

PART FIVE

Andy Keller, Oak Grove third baseman

Luke showed me an article
about a college pitcher who was blind in one eye.
He asked me if I'd sent it.
I told him I hadn't,
but if I'd seen it, I *would* have sent it.
"If this guy can do it, you can," I said.

Luke shook his head. "If I were a pitcher, maybe.
But pitching's not the same
as catching fly balls or hitting fastballs."

"You don't know until you try," I said.

"Sure," Luke muttered. "Remember when
Mrs. Trucelli quoted some writer
about the difference between lightning
and the lightning bug?"

"Yeah," I said. "Mark Twain."

"Well," Luke said, "there's a big difference
between *playing* and just playing."

I told Luke he was no Mark Twain,
but I knew what he meant.

Daryl Hucklebee, Oak Grove coach

Sure, maybe I lied just a bit.
But not all lies are bad.
Andy Keller asked me if I would talk to Luke,
let him know it's possible
to play good baseball with just one good eye.
The truth of the matter is, I doubt it.
I've never seen a one-eyed baseball player.

I know the down side—
the problems with depth perception:
picking up the flight of a ball,
the spin on a pitch.
But I wasn't going to focus on the problems.
I told Luke that the loss of an eye
shouldn't keep someone from excelling.
It all comes down to attitude, to mental toughness.
It's mental toughness that helps athletes
overcome physical disabilities.

Who knows? Maybe I'm right.

Michelle Wallace, Luke's mother

Luke seems more upbeat
than at any time since he got hurt.
Part of it, I'm sure, is because he knows
he'll be able to come home soon.

He's been so active his whole life,
and for weeks now he's been stuck in that hospital bed,
barely able to move.
He must feel relieved,
knowing it won't be long before he'll be outside,
running around again.

The doctor said if everything goes as expected,
Luke should be able to resume normal activities
in a few weeks.
His only limitations will be those imposed
by his impaired vision,
and he'll just have to find out for himself what's possible.

I was so worried,
but now it looks as if I'll have Luke back after all.

Maybe God really was listening.

Larry Wallace, Luke's father

Luke and I talked today.
Really talked.
It was the first time since he's been here
that he's said more than just a few words to me.
He showed me some articles he's been reading.
He told me he thought I'd sent them to him,
but I said I hadn't.

One was about a professional hockey player.
Luke said if someone with only one eye can play hockey,
as fast paced as it is, then maybe it's possible
to play baseball or football or basketball.
"Sure it is," I said. I told him there wasn't any reason
he shouldn't be able to run and swing a bat
and throw a pass and shoot a basketball.

"I don't know," he said. "But I want to give it a try."

Luke "Wizard" Wallace

I just got a visit from Kyle Dawkins.
It was awkward for both of us.
I was alone when he came to my room.

"I'm so sorry, Luke," he said.
Then he also apologized for not coming earlier.
He said he'd been wanting to for weeks,
but he'd always backed out at the last minute.
He said he was ashamed to face me.

I didn't know how to respond.
Ever since that game, I've pictured him in my mind:
6'4" and a solid 220, without an ounce of fat.
I see him staring in before that final pitch,
the ball in his right hand,
gleaming bright red like a fireball.

At least that's my vision of it.
I think of how I could fling my bat at him,
knock him right off the mound
before he can deliver the pitch.
But I've known all along he didn't hit me on purpose.
I've played against him in three sports; he's a decent guy.

"You going to be okay?" he asked.
I thought of a dozen different ways to answer—
none of them nice.
I thought, "I'll be damned if I say something
to make you feel better.
You can hurt a while longer, the way I have to."
But then I looked at him, this powerful athlete,
brushing his hand across his eyes
to wipe away tears.
And finally I said, "Sure, Kyle. I'll be fine.
Don't sweat it, man."

After he left, I wondered if I'd said the right thing.

Andy Keller, Oak Grove third baseman

When Luke told me Dawkins had come to visit him,
I told him about Kyle quitting the Compton team.
Luke hadn't known.
I hadn't told him earlier because I thought
he might not want to hear Kyle's name.

"He quit," Luke repeated.

"Right after it happened," I said.

Luke didn't say anything for a while.
Then, in a voice so soft I could barely hear it,
he said, "It wasn't Kyle's fault.
All along I've been blaming him for throwing at me.
But it was as much my fault as his.
I made a bonehead decision.
I knew how wild he is, but I was leaning in,
expecting an outside pitch.
How long have we been playing ball?
I should have known better. I got careless."

"It wasn't your fault," I said.

Luke bit at his lower lip.
He ran a hand through his hair.
"That's what I should have told Kyle," he said.
"That it wasn't his fault."

"You still can," I said. "You can call him and tell him."

"Maybe I will," he said.

Sarah Edgerton, Oak Grove student

Luke smiled at me today.

I almost didn't go visit him.
I wanted to see him, but I didn't know
what kind of mood he'd be in.
What if he was angry about those articles,
and he found out I was the one who'd sent them?
But I finally decided to go anyway.

His head is still all bandaged, and he still looks bad.
But when I walked in the room,
his face seemed to light up.
He actually seemed glad to see me.
At least he made me feel that way for the first time ever.
I'm so happy I was finally able to make him smile.

Luke "Wizard" Wallace

Sarah came today.
I was hoping she would,
but I wasn't expecting it.
I haven't exactly been great company
when she's been here.

It's a funny thing: when we worked on
that research project at school,
I never thought of her as pretty—
at least not in the way Melody is.

But today . . .
She must have done something different—
with her hair, her clothes.
I don't know.
But when she smiled,
it actually sent a little tingle through me.

Does that sound crazy?

I told her about some of the articles I'd read
about athletes with impaired vision,
and she got a funny look on her face,
as if she felt embarrassed
or guilty about something.

It was as though a light
had been snapped on in my head.

Sarah Edgerton, Oak Grove student

"It was you, wasn't it?" Luke said.

"What was me?"

"You sent me those articles."

I wondered how he knew, or if he was just guessing.
Should I tell him the truth or not? I'm not a good liar.
Before I could say anything,
he read the answer on my face.

"Thanks" he said. "I'm glad you did.
But why didn't you let me know it was you?"

"I didn't want you to be mad at me."

He reached out his hand toward me.
I didn't know what else to do,
so I reached mine toward him.
He squeezed it.
"No way," he said. "I'd never be mad at you."

Gordie Anderson, Oak Grove center fielder

We play Compton tomorrow.
That's always the game we most want to win.
We've lost one conference game, and they've lost four,
but we need to win to stay in first place alone.
Palo Cove has lost two.
A loss to Compton would tie us with them.

More than anything, we want to beat Compton
because of their coach.
He's a real piece of work.
I don't know how his team can play for him.
He'll be coaching at third
and yell at a guy for taking a called strike on the corner.
But if a player swings at one on the corner and misses,
he'll scream at him to be more selective.
I'm surprised anyone on that team has his head on straight.

At least we won't have to face Dawkins.
I feel bad for him; he's a great pitcher.
I guess he quit because of beaning Luke,
but maybe the real reason was that he was fed up
with playing for their bigmouth coach.

I'm sure glad we have Coach Hucklebee.

Red Bradington, Compton coach

If we win only one more game this year,
I sure as hell hope it's this one.
That first Oak Grove game ruined our whole season.
If Dawkins hadn't hit the kid, he'd still be pitching,
and we'd still have a shot at the title.

I get mad every time I think about how
that damn Oak Grove kid froze.
If he'd just gotten out of the way . . .

He ruined our whole damn season.

Kyle Dawkins, Compton pitcher

The last few days have been tough.
With the Oak Grove game coming up,
everybody remembers.

Even if they don't say it out loud,
I can see it in their eyes.
Some of them blame me for our season
going down the crapper.

Pete says not to worry about it.
He says Coach has been making me the fall guy,
and a couple players bought into it.
But most of them didn't.

All I know is, I made the right decision.
When I saw Luke in that hospital bed,
his face all bandaged up
and blind in one eye because of me,
I knew I was right
not to risk doing that to someone else.

Pete Preston, Compton catcher

I'm Kyle's catcher, not his shrink.
I can't tell him he should pitch again,
but I think he needs to.
Not for Bradington.
Not even for the team.

For himself.

That's easy for me to say;
I've never been the cause

of anybody getting hurt that bad.
But it was an accident,
and Kyle's got to put it behind him now.

Oh, I understand why he couldn't pitch
right after it happened.
But when I see how it's eating at him, I worry.

I've tried to tell him it wasn't his fault.
He's got a great future as a pitcher
if he gets control—
and I don't mean just of his pitches.
I mean control of his emotions, too.

I'm no shrink; I can't tell him he should pitch again.
He has to tell himself.
I hope to hell he can.

Tim Burchard, umpire

I wish I hadn't gotten assigned to ump
the Oak Grove–Compton game.
Not because of what happened to the Wallace boy.
Because of Bradington.

Most coaches are fine.
Oh, sure, there's always someone upset
at a couple calls every game.
That's expected.

But Bradington—
if he's not yelling at one of the umps,
he's yelling at his own players.

I have to tell you, I earn my money at Compton games.
I can control what he says to me
by threatening to toss him
if he says another word about one of my calls.
But I can't stop him from shouting abuse
at his own players.

I'd never penalize the kids on a team
because of the antics of their coach,
but Compton games make it tough
for any ump to be completely objective
and just call them like he sees them.
A borderline pitch? Sometimes it's a struggle
to ignore which team is Bradington's.

Gordie Anderson, Oak Grove center fielder

Coach Hucklebee's a low-key guy. Never yells much.
But it's funny.
Today he had to chew us out—
for laughing at the Compton coach.
You could tell his heart wasn't in it;
you could see he was trying hard not to laugh himself.
One of the things he preaches is to respect the other team.
But there's no way to respect their coach.

Bradington was ragging on his own players the whole game.
He'd beaten them halfway down already,
so it was easy for us to finish the job.
Only the ten-run rule kept us from stomping on them worse.

Andy Keller's been red-hot with the bat.
He pounded out four more hits today.
I guess he was out to get revenge
for what happened to Luke.

Red Bradington, Compton coach

That damn team of mine.
What a bunch of chokers!
They just flat-out quit on me.
I'm embarrassed to admit I'm their coach.
Teams like this year's make me wonder
why I even bother.
They don't appreciate what I do for them.
All they care about is girls and video games
and cars and who knows what all.

When I was a kid, we played our guts out.
Nowadays, they don't seem to give a damn.

Daryl Hucklebee, Oak Grove coach

We were going good before,
but ever since that win over Compton,
our kids have been on fire.
Every time they take the field,
it's as if they know they'll find a way to win.
Even if we fall behind early, they never lose their poise.
They know they'll find a way to come back.

This is a team that just won't quit.
I know it's a cliché, "Win one for the Wizard" and all that.
But these kids really do feel the need to win for Luke,
as if going the distance this year
will make some kind of sense out of his injury.

It's great to see that kind of selflessness
in high school kids.
I've never coached a team quite like this one.

Andy Keller and Luke "Wizard" Wallace

"I sure wish you could come down to Coolidge
for the games. Be there when we win it."

"Me, too. But at least the local station
will carry our games.
I'll be able to listen to them on the radio."

"Remember, at the start of the season you called it:
State champs. Two more wins and we've got it.
With Paul and Doug throwing, we've got a good shot."

"I wish I could have been a part of it."

"You were. We couldn't have gotten this far
if we hadn't played every inning
with the same intensity and focus
the Wizard would have."

"It's not the same, though."

"I know."

Willard Kominski, longtime Oak Grove baseball fan

Heartbreak.
Oh, this was tough to take. One win away
from going to the state championship game.

The only consolation is, we didn't lose it;
Beva High came out in the seventh and took it from us.

We were just one out away.
Paul Gettys pitched maybe the finest game of his life.
Beva had only one base runner going into the seventh.
We led, 1–0.

Paul struck out the first two. Then they got
a scratch hit and a bloop double.
The next hitter got jammed with a good fastball,
but he punched it to left center.
Gordie raced over and dived for it.
It was a great try, but the ball was just out of reach.

There's an old saying, "If a bullfrog had wings,
he wouldn't bump his rear end."
In other words, it's no good wondering "What if?"

Still, I can't help thinking . . .
if Luke Wallace, the Wizard, had been there,
he might have caught that ball.

Daryl Hucklebee, Oak Grove coach

It was a tough call, picking the MVP.
I had five boys I could have given it to,
and nobody would have complained.
There were the two pitchers:
Paul Gettys and Doug Goulin.
Then there was Andy Keller and Alonzo Mitchell.
Keller gave us a big shot in the arm.
He surprised us all by how well he hit.
He finished at .388, about two hundred points
higher than I would have thought.
Mitchell played a great shortstop and stole more bases
than the rest of the team combined.

But I had to go with Gordie Anderson, our top hitter.
He had big shoes to fill on defense,
taking over in center after Luke got hurt.
Nobody ever forgot the way the Wizard
could handle the glove,
but they all respected the job Gordie did.

Luke "Wizard" Wallace

Dad pulled into the driveway, and there it was:
The house. The basketball hoop. Mom's garden.
I went inside and climbed the stairs.
After weeks of being stuck in bed
and seeing nothing but hospital walls,
walking into my own room,
with all my stuff just the way I'd left it,
was like being reborn.

I looked out the window.
I could see Andy's house across the street, two houses down.
I opened my closet and saw sneakers. Baseball cleats. Clothes.
Real clothes, not hospital gowns.

My mouth was already watering at the thought
of Mom's cooking, and of actually sitting at the dinner table,
instead of eating off a hospital tray.

I realized I'd never really appreciated home before,
not the way a person should.

I realized how close I'd come
to never seeing home again.

Sarah Edgerton, Oak Grove student

I knew Luke would be going home today.
He told me so the last time I saw him, three days ago.
What I didn't expect is that he'd call me
and ask me to go to the movies with him Friday night.
He said he wanted to celebrate his homecoming,
and he wanted to share it with me
because I'd been there for him and kept his spirits up.

He didn't actually tell me he liked me
or say that he wanted me to be his girlfriend or anything.
But that's okay.

I'm going to the movies with Luke Wallace.

Larry Wallace, Luke's father

When Luke asked if I'd play catch with him later today,
I couldn't help but think of when we first
played catch together years ago.
In the beginning, he missed most all of my tosses.
But it didn't take long before his mitt was like a magnet.
Missing a ball was inconceivable to him.

Anything he could get to, he could catch,
and his ability to judge the flight of a ball was uncanny.

I wondered which Luke I'd see today,
the beginner or the magician.

Luke "Wizard" Wallace

I was scared to try,
but I finally did it: I threw some with Dad.

When I followed his first soft throw
all the way into my glove
and somehow caught it clean,
it was like seeing a rainbow after a dark storm.
I'd been afraid I wouldn't be able
to catch the ball at all.

We threw for maybe ten minutes,
normal warm-up type throws.
Even though I caught most of them,
it was hard having to concentrate
and watch the ball all the way.
I felt as if I were wishing it into my mitt.

And all the time I was thinking:
catching easy lobs is one thing;
fly balls, that'll be another story.

Michelle Wallace, Luke's mother

It's so wonderful having Luke home—
and not only home, but, praise the Lord,
having him home with a big smile on his face.
When I think how close we came to losing everything...

I'm the luckiest of mothers.

Luke "Wizard" Wallace

I waited until it was dark; then I walked the eight blocks
to the school baseball field.
It was my first time there since that pitch.
I wanted to make sure I was alone,
because I didn't know how I'd feel.
I didn't know if I'd bawl like a baby
or curse
or who knows what.
But I had to go there.

I had this crazy idea that it was all a bad dream,
that if I went to the field, some kind of time warp
would transport me back to the moment before the pitch.
I'd focus on Kyle's hand,
and when it came forward and released the ball,
I'd fall in the dirt and let the pitch sail harmlessly by.

I'd almost convinced myself I could make it happen.

The moon was full when I walked into the batter's box.
I saw the mound clearly.
I didn't bawl, and I didn't curse.

But I knew right off it hadn't been a dream.

Andy Keller, Oak Grove third baseman

I tried to phone Luke before going over to see him.
His dad said that he'd left a few minutes earlier,
that he'd said he felt like taking a walk.
I figured there were two places where Luke might be.
I didn't include Sarah's house.
I'm not sure exactly where she lives,
but I know it's not within walking distance.
And since Luke hadn't stopped at my house,
I went to the other place.

He was standing at home plate when I got there.
I stayed in the shadows where he couldn't see me
and watched as he slowly walked to first base.
He stepped on it and went on to second.
Then he kept going, right out into center field.
He walked to within ten feet of the fence,
turned, and looked back toward the infield.

When I left, he was still standing there.

Luke "Wizard" Wallace

I had Andy hit me fly balls today.
It was tough.
After playing catch with Dad yesterday
and catching most of his throws,
I'd hoped it would be easier.

It was only Andy and me.
I didn't want anybody else watching us,
in case I made a fool of myself.

I caught most of the high, lazy flies.
But not the line drives.
No matter how hard I tried to focus,
a lot of them got past me before I could react.

I realize I'll never have the knack
for judging balls the way I did before.
Before, the batter swung and I *knew*.
Now, the batter swings and I *hope*.

Andy Keller, Oak Grove third baseman

Luke asked me if I'd drive him to Compton
so he could talk to Dawkins.
I told him I'd drop him off and come back later,
if he wanted a private conversation.
But he said no,

there wasn't anything he planned to say
that I couldn't hear.

So I sat with them and drank one of the sodas
Dawkins brought out.
I hadn't seen him since the game.
He is one big dude—
even bigger than I'd remembered.

As he and Luke talked,
I couldn't help thinking how we had a great season,
even without Luke,
but Compton fell apart after Dawkins left their team.

I wonder why.

Kyle Dawkins, Compton pitcher

Luke Wallace phoned me yesterday
and said he wanted to see me.
How could I say no? I owe him that much.
I owe him whatever he asks of me.

One of his buddies drove him over today.
We sat out in my yard for almost an hour.
Luke said he was going to work out all summer
to get himself back in shape.
He said he planned to play everything next year—
football, basketball, baseball.
He said he was going to try, at least.

He asked where I'd be going to college,
and I told him. I didn't tell him
I wouldn't be playing baseball there.

He said, "I know they'll be glad
to have you pitching for them."
He said, "I hope you have a great season."

After he left, I got out my duffle bag,
the one with all my baseball gear.
I didn't know if I could bring myself
to open it, but I finally did.
I took out a baseball
and wrapped my fingers around the seams.

I held it for a long time.

Luke "Wizard" Wallace

By the time I got home from the hospital,
there were just two weeks of classes left.
My folks talked to Principal Jenks,
and he said I didn't have to go back to school
unless I wanted to. I was glad of that.

There's not much wrong with my face now.
I look normal, and I don't have to
wear an eye patch or anything.
But with final exams coming up,

115

it would've been too distracting
for me to show up at school.
Not just for me, but for the other kids, too.

My teachers had been sending me assignments.
I guess I did enough of them to get by.
I'd gotten some good class notes
from Andy and Sarah and a few other kids.
And while I was in the hospital,
Mom had read my textbooks out loud to me.

It was cool, too, what Jenks did:
he collected all my final exams from my teachers,
and he told Mom she could let me take them at home
under her supervision.

I passed all my classes with a C or better.
At least those are the grades my teachers gave me.
Nobody said as much, but maybe it was their gift
to try to compensate for the loss of my eye.
I didn't ask for that kind of gift,
but if that's what it was, I'm grateful.

Sarah Edgerton, Oak Grove student

"Sometimes I feel guilty," I said to my dad.
"If Luke hadn't gotten hurt,
we probably wouldn't be dating now."
Dad just smiled and shook his head.

He said that Luke's injury
had nothing to do with us starting to date.
He said, "I see the way that boy looks at you,
the way he brightens up when you come into the room.
He would have noticed you soon enough.
His accident was bad luck, no doubt of that.
But it's lucky for him he found you."

Well, what can I say? He's my dad;
he gets carried away sometimes.
But I think he's right.
Luke and I would have found each other eventually.
We can talk to each other, really talk.
And we make each other laugh.
If we were together because either one of us
felt pity or some sense of obligation, I'd know.
We're together because we like each other.
A lot.

I don't know what the future holds,
but the present is plenty nice.
I'm happy with that.

Lisalette Dobbs, Oak Grove student

Andy Keller phoned me and asked
if I'd like to go to a movie with him
and Sarah and Luke.
I was so excited, I barely hung up the phone

before I started whooping,
and Mom gave me that look of hers—
that slight shake of the head and the half smile.

Andy Keller!
All spring I've been hoping he'd ask me out.

Andy Keller, Oak Grove third baseman

Luke and I have been working out together
almost every day since school ended—
running, lifting weights, throwing.

Usually Clarissa practices with us.
I have to admit: for a twelve-year-old,
she's pretty darn good.
She's almost as good at catching fly balls now
as Luke is.
In a way, that's sad;
but I tell myself it's because
Clarissa is showing real talent,
not because Luke is so much worse
than he was before he got hurt.

It's obvious that catching a fly ball
is work for Luke now.
He just can't glide under the ball like he used to.

But he's improving every day,
and even though he says
he'll never be as good as he once was,
I'd never bet against the guy.

Not against Luke.
Not against the Wizard.